Prophet

A NOVEL BY SHULAMITH HAREVEN

Translated from the Hebrew by Hillel Halkin

NORTH POINT PRESS   *San Francisco   1990*

LIBRARY OF CONGRESS CATALOGING-IN-PUBLICATION DATA
Hareven, Shulamith.
    [Navi. English]
    Prophet : a novel / by Shulamith Hareven ; translated
    from the Hebrew by Hillel Halkin.
        p.   cm.
    Translation of: Navi.
    ISBN 0-86547-423-0
    I. Title.
PJ5054.H292N3813   1990
892.4'36—dc20   89-25497

Prophet

1

The ways of the world began to turn upside down about one hour after sunrise. Herds of livestock that should have jostled through the narrow gate, spilling like a slow sea upon the hills, were seen to stop in their tracks, while distant shepherds turned suddenly, rounding up their flocks, and headed back into the city. Quickly they drove, frantically, with much brandishing of staffs, as if the day had been cut short and evening came abruptly, while the light was still new, and the sun warm in the east.

From the gate rose a din of shouts and shoving. Herds mixed with each other and blocked each other's way, some struggling to get out, others clamoring to get back in, cow haunch pressed against sheep flank, in a great teeming vortex. Thick clouds of dust soared all along the ascent to Gibeon, rising very high, as if the earth had suddenly tilted and the road stood up in the air. Cries of shepherds and lashings of prods cut through the continuous bellows and bleats. Kids and lambs were crushed beneath the baffled hooves of jammed cattle, their loud, desperate calls crying doom.

Here and there, on the fringes of the vortex, a few sheep and calves broke free of the dense cluster, and stampeded up the narrow streets, fleeing the tumult and the shouting shepherds, whose staffs failed to make way among the heaving flesh. The city wall was invisible. Scanty light filtered through the swirling columns of dust, sickly, yellow, and apocalyptic.

Worried Gibeonites looked on from the wall and the rooftops. The city was built on the flat top of a steep hill overlooking a fertile, generously sprawling valley of trellised grapevines and olive, pomegranate and carob trees, beyond which lay the land of the Jebusite. It was from there, the Gibeonites told themselves mournfully, it was from the east, from the desert, that the evil would come. They were already said to be close, very close. They might even be behind those straggling sheep, picking off the last strays. Was not that the glint of their spears in the distant dust? The shepherds had seen them with their own eyes; ask the shepherds. A people come upon us from the desert. There would be war. There would be a siege.

The voices dropped to anxious whispers. Get everyone inside the gate, they said, get everyone inside and bolt it shut. As if by themselves, their hands described little worried, enfolding movements.

Children who had awakened and gone outside stood staring open-mouthed at the changed world. Everything was diminished, gathered in on itself. The gatekeepers strove in vain to swing the great gate shut and drive home the corner bolt. The square was waist-high in animals. Slavering cows, rancid-fleeced, burr-infested sheep, the whole apprehensively lowing swarm of life, had brought the fields into the fieldless town. The marketplace, with its large, worn paving stones, the edges of the pool by the water tunnel, which should have been crowded at this hour with launderers and water drawers, were now one quivering mass of beast, dense with heat and smells. Swarms of flies accompanied the animals with an unearthly buzzing, whining and taut like many bowstrings endlessly twanged. Barefoot children pressed into the alleyways, caught up in the squirm of herds. The clowns among them hiked up their tunics and danced with the sheep and cows, bare buttocks rubbing against them, hips gyrating obscenely, faces twisted in laughter, wild with wonder and fright.

Finally the gate was shut halfway, and the living sea backed up into streams, each quickly flowing off into another alley. The square emptied out. Only the sound of tremulous bleating still came from everywhere. Several lambs lay crushed upon the ground among fresh droppings, covered by flies as if by a coat of glistening black fur. The dust settled and the sun shone brightly again.

Hivai wiped his face with the back of his broad hand and descended from the wall. Four of the city elders climbed down heavily with him, supporting themselves on a bowed fig tree that grew from where it had sprouted in the stones of the wall. At once a small band of men surrounded them, some talking quickly, close enough to grip the elders' girdles, others squinting off into the sunlight, too abashed to meet the elders' eyes. The city had no pasture. It had no vegetable gardens. It had no garrison. What should a man do that he might live?

It was so. Even the vegetable patch at the foot of the wall had long been neglected and overgrown by thistles. No one had threatened Gibeon for ages. It was a city as large as a royal capital and it had forgotten what fear was like.

The elders listened and kept silent. They seemed to have no words left. Though they said nothing to Hivai, their quick glances at him were sharp as swords. Prophesy, Hivai. Prophesy, man. Isn't that what you were made for? Speak and tell us what a man should do that he might live, so that we can tell all these people.

Hivai stared at the ground. There was no prophecy in him. The elders' unspoken words struck at him like fists in a bitter, discouraging complaint. Why, they knew very well that he could not prophesy to order. He himself never knew whence his prophecy came or whither his prophecy went. It might fail him for years at a time or come to him twice in one day. Expert at such things though he was, he augured neither by the flight of birds nor by the entrails of sacrifices, nor by the bladders of the muscular fish that the Philistine brought on his she-ass in waterskins from the coast. Nor did he tell fortunes with molten wax poured on water; nor with bowls of wheat sprouts, as did the soothsaying women. All these came from the little gods, from the Asheroth perhaps, or from the virgin sycamore on the outskirts of town whose fruit had never been cut.

Everyone knew its powers. Enfeebled men seeking succor came to it from all over the mountain land, cheered on by its horde of sanctuary harlots.

But prophecy such as that which had come to him, a man in his middle forties, no more than nine or ten times in his life, was not from these. Perhaps it was from the great gods of the north, the gods of Mount Lebanon; perhaps from gods even greater, the gods of the great rivers, beyond which there was nothing, of that far world-root where dwelt the Fathers of All. Yet this too was far from certain. When it came, it was as if a door opened wide and he could remember the future, could recall it as exactly as if it had happened no more than a moment ago. Once he felt that he was earth, all-earth and all-earth-growth, whereupon he remembered with very great awe that there would be a drought. Another time, with a single sharp pang of his flesh, he knew the pain and sickness that would betide every plague-ridden house in the city—knew it while his chest was filled with a great weeping that would not be wept for many days.

When he knew, he told the elders. When he did not, he said nothing. The elders listened thoughtfully. They knew his prophecies always came true.

He would have withstood torture again, if only it would do some good. Years ago, when he was young and did not know his own strength, he had let himself be brought to the temple and forced to prophesy there. He had been plied with wine, with pestled drugs, with incense, with fasts, with sharp rods that tore at his body. And yet he had hardly felt them. Being in the dark, airless temple, which was like being at the bottom of a pit suffused with the smell of blood and smoke, had paralyzed him with fear. At times, through the clouds of incense, he had made out a small child brought to be sacrificed, crying as it held out its arms to its father. He knew he should know who it was and what it meant, but he never did. Sometimes he thought it a fiction, a figment of his own terror, and sometimes, dredged from deep within him, he thought he could remember a fair five-year-old boy whose name he had forgotten, though once he had played with him in the sunshine before losing him in this darkness. Each time he entered the temple, he was sure it had really been so, and that soon, in the next day or even hour, it would come back to him. Yet each time he stepped back into the street, he was no wiser than before. They saw the bafflement in his face, the torment to know, and persisted.

9

Prophesy, Hivai. Prophesy, man. Their low, muffled voices weighed him down. To remember. To know. To remember. To know.

This time, too, he would have undressed without a murmur, baring the long welts of flesh that were left on his back from those days. He had never protested; he had submitted to the rack as if desiring it, so great was his longing for the moment of prophecy, for that opening forth in which the memory of the future became clear. Apart from these rare times of liberation, his life had the plodding gait of an ox that walks the straight furrow of time from the Was to the Will-be. Even when his torturers despaired of him, he continued sordid self-torments of his own in the hope of success. Yet no door opened. Time would not turn about. Nothing he said when drugged made any sense. His babblings when beaten failed utterly to come true; far from enhancing his reputation, they faded away like so much smoke. Until at last Yeremoth and Shaham consulted and gave the order to desist. It would come when it was ready.

The elders turned their eyes from him and went their way. The small band of men scattered too.

Although the morning was still young, Hivai felt a leaden roof of fatigue descend on him. Slowly he walked along the wall, crossed the culvert that ran out of the city, and continued on his way. The wall looked different. Many men stood on it, shading their eyes to peer out into the distance. The enemy was not to be seen.

Large and lanky, he ambled on toward the pool. The marketplace was changed too. Three or four groups of strangers sat between its stalls with their belongings, breaking bread with their children. Refugees from some outlying farm, he thought, wondering wearily who had let them in. Perhaps they had tricked the guards, or stolen in with their flocks, tying themselves under the rams' bellies. Who could know? With the insolence of despair, they had spread their faded mats and sat down to eat, installing themselves, confident that no one would drive them away. The idol vendors in the marketplace glanced covetously at them and their bundles. As Hivai passed by, one of their children reached out and grasped his foot, smiling up at him from the damp pavement, his cheeks bronzed like a pomegranate. Hivai kicked free, and the child let out a solitary whimper. Yeremoth will have them killed, he thought. The idol vendors did not budge.

Annoyed at himself, he kept walking, as if to inspect, or protect, the city. Its weakest point was in the north.

Here the houses were few, and the slope beneath them fell away in a thicket of bushes and nettles that were dusty-dry from the summer. Fig trees sprawled over the rocks. The winter had been rainy, and the harvest was abundant. Hivai followed a narrow path that led to the northern wall, treading on the rank caper plants that grew out of an abandoned stone fence. Swarms of bees reveled round him like wedding guests.

He spat the last dust from his mouth. The figs will whore too, he thought moodily: strangers will pick them and eat them while our corpses litter the rocks. Gibeon suddenly seemed wide open, insubstantial, an illusion more than a city: a man need only lean against its wall, or shout aloud, or sound a ram's horn, and everything would come tumbling down. Would that his arms were walls.

The jug in front of Bagbag's house was turned upside-down, signifying a visitor. He hadn't meant to visit her, yet after striding on a bit over ground strewn with rotten figs, broken pottery, and garbage, he changed his mind. He would go see her and chase away the whelp inside, he thought, finally finding an object for his anger. He would take him by the scruff of his neck and toss him out.

But when he stooped to let his tall frame through the

low doorway, the visitor was already carefully adjusting his cloak and belt. Hivai did not know the man, a stranger who made himself so inconspicuous that he was all but invisible, unlike the local Canaanite dogs, who hadn't the least notion of manners. Without favoring him with a glance, Hivai strode into the small room, filling it with his bulk while his eyes grew accustomed to the darkness.

Two narrow windows let in a bit of light, which fell in patches on a worn purple rug. A small tallow candle in a wall niche was doubled by its reflection in a coaster of hammered copper. Old, tired, and rheumy-eyed, Bagbag sat on a pile of ancient rugs and scraps of wool, trying to clean up some honey that had spilled from a broken jar on the floor. Before Hivai could sit, she seized him by his cloak, gripping it tightly. What should a man do that he might live? Tell me, Hivai. What.

She burst into tears when he asked her what the matter was, agitatedly wiping her nose, from one nostril of which hung a large ring. They'll slit our throats, she wailed. We'll be butchered like sheep on a feast day. I tried to read the honey and saw blood.

He railed at her foolishness. The strength of his anger frightened her into ceasing her sobs. Blinded by tears, she collapsed on her knees before him by the piles of rugs, hands webbed with the golden honey that also stuck to her sleeves. She rooted for his private parts like an infant seeking the breast, murmuring as she fumbled for them, what will become of us, Hivai, tell me what. You're a prophet, surely you know.

So she too expected him to prophesy, he thought. Was there anyone left in Gibeon who did not clutch at his cloak?

Bagbag kept talking quickly, her hands busy. Ben-Nerbaal had been to see her that morning, she said. Ben-Nerbaal had told her to go to Ai. Ben-Nerbaal had said that Ai was stronger than Gibeon.

If that's what Ben-Nerbaal told you, he said crossly, why don't you go there? His seed spurted out quickly, without pleasure.

Should I? She lifted to him eyes full of sly hope. Should I go to Ai, O prophet?

He tore himself away from her kneading, honeyed hands, threw her a coin, and strode back out into the sunlight. Four or five of the clowning children were waiting outside, eyes painted and cheeks rouged just like Bagbag's, hands mimicking hers to his face. Did she milk some prophecy from you, Hivai? piped one of them as he passed.

He didn't look at them. Turning, he walked back into the city, to be met again by the loud buzzing of the flies that had gone on annoyingly all morning, and by the fractured bleats of the sheep, each time coming from somewhere else, though at this hour they shouldn't have been heard in the city at all.

All that day, and the next day too, the city was not as it had been. The Gibeonites were helpless, diminished; small groups of them huddled together, hands raised contentiously, imploringly. The circles they walked in kept shrinking, as if the siege were already upon them, within the walls, in the streets, in every house. One mustn't stray too far. It was dangerous. They stuck close to the city wall. Their speech lessened too.

Every now and then some young boy came dashing from the wall, shouting they're coming, they're coming, until his wild laughter and that of his friends, scampering away for dear life, informed the townsmen that once again they had been made the butt of a joke. Angry men ran after the boys to thrash them. The boys escaped every time.

The enemy was not to be seen. Nothing stirred in the bushes on the mountains; no campfires flickered there at night. Only the cattle egrets still sailed low above the valley, looking for the missing cows. Four army veter-

ans stood before a house, rubbing old shields with tallow and passing the rust-eaten head of a spear through
a fire. Half of the men watching them claimed that the
fire was too hot, and half that it was not hot enough.
The odor of rust mingled with the smell of tallow already rancid from the sun. Nearby an elderly man
looked on, telling old war stories. At first the others listened; then they spat. The fellow was baking stones for
supper, grinding water at the mill. There hadn't been
a war in Gibeon since the days of their great-grand-
fathers.

The days went by. No one went out to the fields, neither the women to gather kindling nor the men to tend
the crops and trees. On Yeremoth's orders the gate was
kept shut. Gangs of men roamed the city, accosting the
women; yet their hearts were not in it, they simply
went through the motions, a single sharp word sent
them flying. Here and there down some street, beneath a leafy carob or fig tree, groups of idlers sat
playing bones, their laughter sudden and harsh. The
clowning children were everywhere, marching up and
down the steps like ludicrous squads of soldiers with
swords made of hawthorn branches, until the elders
chased them off with curses that rattled like lethal
stones down the sloping streets. People complained

that the summer was the hottest ever, hot and oppressive without end. Only the women still went about their business, bent silently over their housework, hiding their fear, which grew from day to day in a great silence.

The enemy was not to be seen. Once or twice some of the more daring shepherds took their flocks out to pasture beneath the city wall, less than a stone's throw away from it, struggling to keep their balance on the steep slope; but the guards quickly drove them back in. Those are Yeremoth's orders. Why don't you ask Yeremoth, perhaps he will not refuse you. The shepherds stood there timidly, shuffling their feet, not a word in their dry mouths. They were afraid to ask Yeremoth. Back in the city with their flocks, they went to bed at high noon, pulling their heavy cloaks up over their heads to shut everything out.

Little by little the goods disappeared from the marketplace. At first the burdenless porters still hung around, empty-handed and straight-backed as they had not been for years, regarding each other with slow wonder. There had never been time for it before. Unused to such idleness in the middle of the day, they stood waiting for something to happen. The days were marked by small panics, each shout causing fright, each donkey's bray making them jump, until the tension was dispelled by embarrassed laughter. Yet though they mocked one another's fears, all were afraid. Those with anything worth stealing hid it in their houses, in their storerooms, in their cellars, or else cached it in the rocky ground at night, covering the spot with large stones. Women wrapped their jewelry and buried it when no one was looking, hurriedly sticking a branch in the freshly dug earth to make it look like a new sapling. Little was bought, little sold. The stalls of the idol vendors were deserted, their business gone from the edges of the pool: no graven images were left for sale, not even gold. The men stood in the empty marketplace in groups, uncertain what they were doing there. Then they stopped coming. The market is dead, they said. The sun alone still filled its empty spaces, baring the cracks in its grooved paving stones and their streaks of grime.

The days went by. One day some men announced that they were going out to the fields beyond the wall to bring back grain and fruit. They left in the middle of the night and never returned. In the morning the bodies of two guards were found by the gate, run through by daggers. Large flies were already swarming over their rigid jaws. Yeremoth came to the gate in person, looked at his slaughtered men, and walked angrily away. Yeremoth will catch the murderers, it was said in the city. He will skin them alive.

But the departed men's households brazened it out. Their sons, they claimed, had gone to meet the enemy far from the city; they had taken the war to the enemy and would fight to save Gibeon and its inhabitants. More and more people began to spread this story. In one family's house a spit was set up, a calf slaughtered, and meat handed out in the street. The town cheered its heroes and brought their families gifts: honey, branches of sycamore, packets of myrtle, coins, little blue stones brought by the Philistines from the south. The hands of the proud fathers were kissed for the merit of having a savior of the city for a son. Behind their backs, people laughed and winked. They knew the departed men had gone to Ai. Ai was strong. The only necks they had saved were their own.

Now the guards were afraid to man the gate at night. Halfway through the first shift they slipped away to their homes, where they burrowed into their cloaks, blankets, and quilts and slept until the stars grew pale. Slaves and hirelings were stationed in their place. Since no one walked the streets at night for fear of the enemy, the subterfuge went unnoticed. Those who lived near the gate could hear the sounds of reveling until dawn, of drunken voices and bleating women echoing among the large stones.

The days went by. The sun grew milder; there were more and more clouds, their heavy shadows moving upon the mountains like legions on the march. Summer ended quickly, as if cached away too. Longingly they watched the fruit in the valley rot on the trees, dropping to be eaten by great clouds of raucous birds that arrived with the eastward-racing clouds in the sky, wave beneath rippling wave, rising, falling, swirling in endless circles. Flocks of incessantly crying starlings invaded the city, swarming over trees, rooftops, hedges, and ridgepoles until driven off with clubs and much banging of pots and pans. With the autumn breeze came the smell of rotted grapes, as heady as wine, and the fierce, sweet, cloying odor of ripe figs. Summer was over. The city was barricaded tight.

People complained day and night and learned to live with their complaints. No one rebelled. The millstones continued to grind. Large jars of olive oil stood against the walls and all the storerooms were full of lentils and beans. And yet people stared at the full jars and sacks as if looking right through them. There will be hunger, they said; it isn't far off. Sometimes they stole a glance at Hivai as he passed. Perhaps he had some prophecy at last. Perhaps he knew what no one else in Gibeon could know.

No prophecy came. Day and night he tormented himself, tossing sleeplessly in bed, wringing his hands, wishing he were dead. Nothing happened. When he walked in the street, he looked straight ahead and ig-nored all greetings, seeing no one, stopping for no one, letting no one ask him any questions. They stared at him reproachfully, as if he and he alone should be the one to know.

Autumn brought contention. Cut off from their pas-ture, the herds, having eaten all the fodder in the store-rooms, began raiding the gardens by the houses, gob-bling bean and chickpea and celery and the soapwort planted by the housewives between hedges. The black goats were the worst, devouring not only fruits and greens but the very bark off the trees, which they stripped with an unstoppable hunger. The whole city became one great hunger of goats. Thatch roofs van-ished from the low houses, leaving their occupants shivering at night; whole rows of vegetables suddenly disappeared as if the autumn wind had swept them away; onions were rooted from the ground, whether by hoof of beast or secret hand, no one knew.

Anger stalked the houses. A woman seized a sharp spike and killed her neighbor's cow for eating her squashes. A man brutally thrashed his own brother for stealing broad beans from the man's wife. Soon the whole city will be a desert, cried the women. Soon it will be a wilderness. Come see the mighty citadel of Gibeon turn into a land of jackals. They looked for Shaham to judge them, but Shaham was not to be found. No one knew where he was. Some said he had gone to Michmash. Some said to Azekah. Perhaps he would return soon.

Every day at noontime the novice priests paraded out of the temple, flagellating themselves with stone-tipped, brass-studded whips until they bled. Singing in low voices to the rhythm of the lashes, they went from street to street, regarded in silence from the doorways, they and their ominous chant: one-and-two, one-and-two. Skin flayed on half-naked bodies, they would swoop down without warning on one of the houses, from which came a heaven-rending cry. Often a man ran after them into the street, tearing his hair and pleading with them to take his son if they must, but to leave him his fattened calf. Begetting sons was easy, but what prophet, priest, or elder could replace a prize calf? . . . Yet the priests never gave back their prey. Nor did they stop chanting. Thin and agile, their whips thwacking one-and-two on their brightly oiled skin, they marched back to the temple, leaving only their brusque laughter behind them.

Stench began to spread too. At first dead dogs and poultry were thrown over the wall, decomposing where they lay. One morning, however, a woman died in childbirth and a man of old age. Gibeon was built on outcrops of solid rock, lumps of hardened gray with hardly any earth on them. Afraid to bury the dead outside the wall, they kept the corpses at home. No one knew what to do with them. The hired keeners sat by the virgin sycamore, not knowing when to begin or end their dirge. No one bothered to dismiss them. A great unease descended on the city whose dead lay waiting at home. All night the voices of the keeners were heard in the sleepless town. The crying of children awakened the dogs, and the howls of dogs awakened the donkeys and cows, each renewed outburst taking a long while to subside.

One day Hivai went looking for Shaham, striding forcefully as if squashing something with each step, his cloak over his nose to shut out the stench. If Shaham had gone to Michmash, he thought, then from Michmash he would bring him back. He would bring him back from the mountains of Lebanon if he had to, by the scruff of his neck, and sit him down and make him judge the people.

Fists clenched, he stormed into Shaham's house adjoining the wall, almost kicking in the door. Two or three women fled quickly to the attic, veiling themselves with their shawls. He was about to follow them, when some plaits of dried garlic stirred beneath the wattle ceiling, and Shaham emerged from behind them. His beard was unkempt, he wore a coat to keep warm, and in his right hand he held a smoking censer, which he swung back and forth against the malodor as the Gibeonites had learned to do. He did not bother to greet his visitor, but simply stood, flapping his arms with great anger like a demented bird. Of course there was no justice in the city. How could justice be dispensed when the enemy was at the gate? How could there be slave or master or man of might before the law, when tomorrow the enemy might come and make masters of the slaves? If it was true, as Hivai said, that the people were killing each other for a handful of chickpeas, then this too was from the gods, and he, Shaham, was blameless. If Hivai wanted justice so badly, he could judge the people himself. He, Shaham, was not leaving his house. Unless, that is, he went to Ai. Ai was stronger than Gibeon; tonight, indeed, if there was still any respect for an elder in the city, he would order the gate opened and depart. And if Hivai said another word about justice, he might reflect on the fact that not only justice was missing in Gibeon but prophecy too. Let him go to the marketplace and prophesy instead of wasting his time. Let him prophesy to the wind, or to the tree, or to anything he wished. Let the people know what a man should do that he might live.

No prophecy came.

Hivai's family, too, looked at him expectantly. So did the neighbors. So did the man who had paid a bride-price for his son, now trapped between the walls of the city, unable to bring his bride home. So did he who had bought a field and he who had given a loan against the wool of the lender's sheep. It did no good to lock the door against them; their silent beseechings assailed him through the walls. You're a prophet, Hivai. Tell the people, that they may know.

That evening, unable to bear the muteness of the heavens any longer, Hivai seized a small slave child with his left hand, carved out his bowels with his right hand, and dumped the steaming mess in the street to scrutinize. Through the gaseous fumes he clearly made out the crenellated walls of Ai.

A surge of wild joy gripped the city. Some men ran quickly and fell upon the refugees camped by the pool, whose sudden screams were quickly silenced; in their bowels, too, a city was sighted, stone piled heavenward on stone. Ai, it could only be Ai.

All Gibeon seemed to be outdoors. Here and there little fires of thornbushes burned between the houses, making the whole city flicker, casting light and shadow on people by turn. Eagerly, almost with relish, they described the stabbing of the Philistine fishmonger who had been stranded in the city since the locking of the gate. He had had a woman in Gibeon, whom he visited each time he came with his fish-laden donkey, and it was in her house that his murderers had found him. The man was hairy, with a chest like a fur coat, out of which the blood spurted as though from a spring ringed by creepers. In vain had the woman tried to staunch his blood with rags before running outside so that she would not see his death. Other men, it was said, had attacked the home of the Canaanite fortune-teller, killing her and looting her household gods, each leaving with a figurine beneath his cloak. Tomorrow, joked the Gibeonites, the idol vendors would do a brisk trade. The marketplace would come to life again.

A band of rouged and painted children, their lips

very red, their wide eyes lined with antimony, went with the killers to show them other houses. There, over there, that's the house of the hired hand from Azekah. The wife of the man who lives here comes from Ramah. That's the place of the slave from Beth-Horon.

The man from Azekah was found in the wool fuller's house, which was burned to the ground with him in it. The acrid stink of charred felt and wool hung all night above the city, mingling with fetor from the temple. The wool fuller went along with the mob, his mouth agape as he watched all he owned go up in flames. He did not protest.

Standing in the dark streets, their faces aflicker, the others gave their assent. Dry-mouthed, they declared that the killers had done well to dispatch the foreigners. They had brought the evil eye on the city and its inhabitants; they had sucked its lifeblood like so many leeches, eating its food and drinking its water. Let the enemy appear at the gate and they would join him at once.

The thornbushes crackled in the flames. Slowly, their nostrils tickled by the smoke, the Gibeonites inhaled the good, familiar smell, and felt reborn. All summer long they had been utterly worthless; sluggardly, silent, ineffectual. Now autumn had come, and with it fire and night. Now was the time to show no mercy to those who deserved none and to remove the curse from the city. Now was the time to be Gibeonites. They were their old selves again, once more they felt that they were men. The whole city talked of nothing else.

Hivai entered his home and called for his daughter Sahali. It was already two years—from her twelfth birthday—since she had replaced her mother in his bed. Her thin, sun-bronzed, extravagantly bejewelled hands with their acornlike thumbs drove his body wild. He even liked it when she sobbed, liked it better than the way his other women lay beneath him as patient as cattle.

Once Sahali's mother had approached him, openly obsequious. Might she be struck down by lightning if she did anything to anger her lord, whose slightest aggravation she wasn't worth; yet since the day he had graciously honored Sahali by elevating her to his bed, she had gone around like a queen with her anklets, bangles, and rings, lording it over her mother and sisters. She refused to do the least bit of housework; might her mother, Hivai's maidservant, hope to die if it weren't true.

Hivai listened in silence. Then he beat Sahali,

though not hard enough to spoil her looks. He beat her mother, too, to teach her not to bear tales. Sahali laundered, spun, and fetched water as before, a sickly shadow of what she had been.

Now she came, jangling her anklets and chewing on an almond, her many braids dripping oil. Listlessly, without removing the almond from her mouth, she undid her dress. He looked at her sharply: she was as lifeless as a shepherd's fire that has been rained on all winter.

He asked if she too was afraid of the approaching invaders. She nodded.

Then and there he made up his mind. Had he himself not seen Ai in the bowels of the child?

He told her to saddle up the donkey, take two of the servant boys, and set out with them for Ai. And to be sure to keep her face veiled, so that no one in the city would recognize her.

Redoing her dress, she was gone with a bound, as if suddenly resurrected. He understood her haste only too well. But though it was like a stab in the heart, he did not change his mind.

That night he wrapped himself in a large sheepskin coat and went to walk them to the gate. In the house Sahali's mother was wailing, gouging her cheeks and tearing her hair so as not to be accused of rejoicing in her daughter's departure. At the door she kissed her again and again, throwing herself on the doorstep and tearfully seizing the girl by the ankles until Hivai kicked her roughly and ordered her back inside.

It was very dark. The sky was overcast. The donkey's hoofs pattered on the stones like thin rain. One of the servant boys glanced at the sky and predicted rain soon. No one answered.

The hired guards at the gate recognized Hivai at once. Servilely, they hurried to open the stile for him. The dark square with its stone walls as high as the sides of a well were strewn with empty jugs and rags that stank of vomit. The three cloaked figures and the donkey descended the steep slope without looking back. Once the donkey slipped on a wet rock, but one of the boys caught it and helped it laboriously back to its feet. No doubt Sahali had loaded it with more than she had been told she might take.

They vanished in the mist and Hivai turned and walked back. The rain beat down harder. He let the large drops run down his face without wiping them away.

It rained for days and days, and even when it stopped the rain echoed on, dripping from every tree and clump of reeds to trickle through the silent night. The Gibeonites retreated indoors. Many brought in their livestock from their pens, huddling by their sides to keep warm. Mornings, when the fog lifted, the wet boulders shone so whitely in the light that there was no telling where they ended and the clouds began. The low winter sky seemed to have trapped the light between it and the earth in a single pale, horizontal plane. The bad smell was diluted; at times it was possible to breathe pure air. Here and there it was said that the enemy might not come at all, that perhaps the curse had been removed from the city when all the foreigners were killed. It was they who had put an evil spell on Gibeon. Perhaps the enemy had struck out for another city, and they could soon go back to their old ways. Tomorrow or the day after, people said, the gates would be opened again. They slept better too.

Not for long, though. One morning the lookout came running from the tower to shout excitedly, almost incoherently, that it was upon them: a band of men was coming up the road from Beth-Horon, in no time they would be upon the city.

Quickly men climbed the wall to see the enemy. But it was not the enemy at all. There was no glint of armor, no flash of spear in the sunlight that pierced the dark clouds. Little by little the arrivals could be made out more clearly. There were about twenty of them, tired and miserable, barely limping along as if they had been on the road for many days. Two of the youngest reached the gate first. Imploringly, they looked up at it, beards angled toward the sky. They were, they said, from Ai. The invader had put the city to the sword. Of all its men, women, and livestock, only they had escaped with their lives. Would that the sons of Gibeon might open the gate and give them a place to rest their heads. Were not the Gibeonites brothers? Then let them be saviors, too.

Yeremoth, tense and loud, ordered the gate kept shut. Then he went out to the newcomers through the stile, clambering quickly over the rocks. Keeping his distance, he let no one clutch the hem of his cloak, or slip a pleading hand through his belt, or make any claim on his hospitality. From the high rock on which he stood he announced in a stentorian voice that there was no food or water in Gibeon. Let the refugees from Ai go where they wished; let those meant to live, live, and those meant to die, die, and Gibeon be free of blame. He turned back toward the city, a mighty figure, oblivious of the desperate cries for help. The guards made sure to lock the stile well behind him.

For several days the refugees remained on the plateau beneath the wall, begging to be taken in. Some of them were obviously sick, lying slack-jawed on the wet rocks, their gaze averted from the city as if it were not there. Their wretchedness was all that spoke for them. The Gibeonites stood on the wall, looking down on them without a word.

Then the survivors from Ai collected their bundles, helped the sick to their feet, lifted their small children to their shoulders, and straggled off toward Beth-Horon. The plateau before the city was deserted again. Only the wind blew over the rocks, scattering bits of shrubs and bushes long uprooted from their native earth.

A few of the Gibeonites, as if frightened by their own fear, began telling one another in low voices that they did not believe Yeremoth. Indeed, had anyone gone with him outside the gate to make sure that the strangers were from Ai? Could the Aians be told by horns on their heads, or by having three hands instead of two? Ai was too strong to fall to any enemy. The refugees were not from there. Yeremoth had made it all up.

Most vociferous was a certain albino, who stood by the pool with tufts of bleached hair clinging to his neck, his face very red. All morning he told whoever cared to listen that Yeremoth had lied, that he had shamelessly sought to mislead them. He was a Canaanite dog, Yeremoth was, afraid that the Gibeonites would open the gate and desert the city for Ai. That was why, seeing a few last stragglers from the countryside, a ragtag and bobtail of goatherds and smithy's slaves, he had said they were refugees from there. Refugees from Ai, indeed! It was enough to make a person laugh. Ai's walls were as high as the heavens; they were standing to this day. The giant had yet to be born who could conquer Ai.

Gradually, people gathered around the albino, some moved by old grudges, others by anger, hatred, or fear. They stood violently bunched together, spitting at Yeremoth's name. The son of a dog was tricking them all. Not an inch had fallen of Ai, not one. The Gibeonites had slept so long with their cattle that they had become like cattle themselves, believing every lie Yeremoth told them. It was time to rise up as one man, to open the gate and go to Ai and be saved.

Yeremoth's guards dispersed them with clubs, but that still did not make them believe him. They could feel that the blows were not what they might have been, as if the clubs, too, were infected with doubt.

34

Swollen with insolent triumph, the albino went home, a fawning retinue in his wake. The guards looked the other way.

Hivai believed. Ever since the refugees' arrival, his world had caved in on him. His head in his hands, he sat for long hours at home, his jaws working as if chewing the bitter taste of it: a false prophet. Suddenly, that was what he was. Not that it wasn't Ai he had seen in the bowels of the child. He had surely seen it; but he had misunderstood the portent. Such was the way of the little gods: they showed the supplicant enough of the truth to seduce him and played him for a fool. They mocked him, confounded him, just like the clowning children.

Yet he had withstood torture. He had withstood intoxication. The thick welts on his back were his witness. He had withstood everything but his own impatience. He had let himself be gulled like an ordinary fool, rushing to embrace a mirage with outstretched arms like a calf running to its mother's teats. What, after all, had the great gods wanted from him? Only that he wait, that he wait until he knew. But he could not wait. He had played them false, and now they had abandoned him forever.

35

He had seen Ai in the bowels of the child. With his own eyes he had seen it. But the prophecy had not been about the strength of Ai's walls. It had been about their weakness. Ai had fallen. The birds had pecked the flesh of Sahali.

2

Five old men walked in the valley, bundles on their backs, their nostrils flared to inhale the clean air and fresh scents. The rain had stopped overnight and large patches of light drifted over the wet earth like wind-blown fleece. Light poured through the tangled branches of an oak tree, sparkled on the skeins of a spiderweb, cast its blinding cloak on cassia and terebinth, reducing all colors to one. The trees were silent after their flurried night. Twittering calls of birds echoed everywhere. The scents in the air could not be breathed enough of, as though with each breath a man added years to his life. The sleek trees were the essence of freshness; the very stones, washed of their film of dust, seemed to breathe.

It was beyond them why they had not thought of it

before. At first they bore themselves with dignity, as city elders should; yet no sooner were they out of the sight of the watchers on the wall than their steps began to quicken. By the time they reached the shepherds' well, they were almost running, slapping one another's backs and laughing uncontrollably. Out of breath, they pushed aside the well stone with its cover of thorny branches and drew the pure water, drinking and clamoring for more. They had not drunk anything as good in many a month, for the pool in Gibeon had long turned brackish, and it had not yet rained enough to cleanse it.

They wet their heads and beards and splashed each other with water. At last, gasping, gurgling, soaking wet, and drunk with freshness, they sat themselves on the ground. Some last grapes and pomegranates hung from the branches, and they wolfed them down quickly, dripping juice on beards and sleeves. Ben-Nerbaal hung clusters of grapes on his ears and wagged his head slowly, while they all howled with laughter and called him Bagbag. Divlat shut his eyes and folded his hands on his belly like a pregnant woman. Each mind was crossed by the wistful thought that perhaps they need go no further. Perhaps they should stay right here, in this valley, until it was all over, siege, besiegers, and besieged.

Hivai sat off to the side, staring unseeing ahead. Since the arrival of the refugees from Ai, he had taken to blinking as if he were half-blind. Nothing was clear any more. His secret was his gaoler. If called by name, he didn't answer; if shaken, he awoke only partly from his trance. His mouth moved constantly, as if he were chewing.

The elders didn't even look his way. Only yesterday they had still been in Gibeon, their nostrils full of its stench, the brazen glances of the albino and his sycophants accompanying them everywhere. The clowning children had mimicked them mockingly, derisively. And though the taunts had died down each time Yeremoth's guards passed by with their big whips, the grumbling had never stopped. The elders knew well that if they did not take some action, not a stone of their houses would be left standing.

No one remembered whose idea it had been first. Until then the deliberations had been weary. No one knew what to advise, no one seemed to have a shred of wisdom left. It was Harsan who, furrowing his brow, remarked after a while that the invaders' god was born in the desert, whereas the gods of Gibeon were from the mountains. That was why he was a mystery to them. Perhaps he was related to the gods of Egypt.

They said nothing. There was nothing to say. The Egyptians, too, had come and gone. The mountains had conquered them also. Whatever did not turn into mountain itself was soon expelled.

Another while passed and Ben-Nerbaal pointed out that the god of the invaders was a youngster. That was what made him so strong. And the gods of Gibeon were old.

Morosely, they took their time to consider that. Ben-Nerbaal was right. Their own gods were old, they were no longer what they used to be. What had been gained by all the choice bulls and fat lambs and firstborn sons offered up to them? The gods of Gibeon had dined on the town's best beef and mutton and now they were not there when they were needed, they were past their prime, perhaps they were even dead. Or perhaps they had absconded like the swindling Philistine traders, whose tricks everyone knew. They took your money and in the morning they were gone, and with them the goods they had sold you—and what good was your hue and cry then?

At last Shaham spoke up. Slowly, clearing his throat

as if from much cogitation, he declared: If their god is too young and brave to be defeated in battle, perhaps he is untutored enough to be fooled. Suppose we talked him into an alliance; would not Gibeon be saved?

They looked at him in amazement. Never in their lives had they heard anyone suggest that a strong god might be fooled. Petty trickery, of course, was something they knew all about. More than one Gibeonite kept his wealth buried in the earth to outwit the taxman. At calving and lambing time, when the priests came to take the firstborn, they would hide the infant livestock in bushes and caves and pretend it had been a bad year. We must have sinned, they would tell the priests. The young have been carried off by plague. Perhaps we shall be better blessed next year.

Shaham's counsel, however, was of an entirely different nature. It was beyond their capacity to understand. Or to believe in. Were they seriously expected to dupe the invaders' god by a ruse any shepherd lad could see through? Why, they would simply make a laughingstock of themselves. How small today was Shaham's wisdom, they exclaimed, how small and uninspired.

But Shaham, having spoken his mind, waited in triumphant silence, his beard pointing stiffly, his old

eyes half-shut like a turtle's. No one could think of anything better. Gradually, as if getting used to a new dish
that neither they nor their fathers had ever tasted, they
began to accept what he had said. Each looked to the
other for assurance. Perhaps it might work after all.
Perhaps.

Only Harsan objected. We'll be their captives, he
grumbled. Captivity, replied Shaham with a shake of
his head, is a death you live to tell about.

Their spirits rose. All could feel how eager they were
to set out. No man was wiser than Shaham, no counsel
better than his. They would go forth from Gibeon to
make sport of the invaders. The wisdom of Gibeon's elders would vanquish the boy-god and save the city.
Yeremoth alone, it was decided, would remain behind
with his guards, whose big whips would ensure law
and order until their return.

Now, though, having set out, return was far from
their minds. In the valley bathed in afternoon light, all
such considerations appeared distant. Gone was the
stench, which their clothes had shed only slowly, and
with it the whole moldy, smelly, whining, noisy city,
bleating dirges by night and rolling tangles of brawls
from street to street by day. In the clean air and great silence they felt born anew. Their feet led them over the

saddle of the almost bald ridge, where amid rocks nothing but a few cassia bushes and nettles grew. A welcome breeze blew and they walked bunched together, conversing. At the top of the ridge, Harsan climbed a bit further to get a better look. Shading his eyes, he looked in all directions before clambering back to join them. As far as the horizon, there was not a soul to be seen.

Slowly the sun sank westward, gilding the branches of the tall cypress trees scattered over the mountain. A flock of storks circled above them in the last light, rising back into the sky each time they touched the treetops, as if afraid to land. In the crystal-clear air, they could see very far. They stopped to take in the view, the worry lines smoothed from their faces as if by the first sunset of their lives. Hivai alone did not bother to look. Tall, but bent as though beneath a heavy burden, he trailed after them with his eyes lowered, seeing only the swiveling hips of the man ahead of him. He did not answer when spoken to, and after a while he was spoken to no more.

The autumn day faded suddenly. A cold wind blew from the west, cutting icily through the rags they wore. Unsure which direction to head in, they bunched more closely together and came to a halt.

With the cold came dejection, the melancholic blast of night. Though they were still near Gibeon, they felt far indeed from its candles and warm hearths. Who knew if they would return? There might be no way back. Or no Gibeon. Or no tomorrow.

Harsan signaled them to climb in his direction. Ascending a bit higher up the rocky slope, they came to a dry cave, its floor covered with dry old animal droppings. A carob tree hid the entrance, its branches so thick that the bushes beneath it had hardly been wetted by the rains. When the sun vanished and the world was gone for the day, they made a fire, laboring over its sparks as if breathing new life into themselves, fighting the fear that crept up the gnarled veins of their legs into their cold, bony knees, the knees of men who were old.

The fire was finally started. They sat around it warming their hands, then took some sprigs of chickpeas from their packs and roasted them in the coals. Smoke filled the chimneyless cave, and they lay coughing. Their talk was cut short by the darkness, which dispelled the closeness among them and turned each man in on himself.

Lying at a distance from the others, Hivai watched one or two of them rise and shake the fleas from his coat into the flames. They did not dare go far from the cave and urinated right outside it, stepping with a small, embarrassed laugh over the body of the prophet blocking the exit. After a while no one talked or stirred, and there was nothing but coughs, farts, snores, and a few last popping sounds of burrs exploding in the cinders.

It took Hivai a long time to fall asleep. Trapped by his secret, he was frightened even of sleep. He lived through the days in a fog, like a man wading through water, but the nights gripped him with terror. He feared the vengeance of the great gods as he had never feared anyone or anything in his life. Another day or two, another night, and it was sure to overtake him, hard and inevitable. He had no idea whether his death would be sudden, or if life would drain slowly out of him, ever so quietly, like the blood from slit veins, until sight faded, breathing ceased, heart beat for the last time. Had there been anyone to turn to, he would have turned. Had there been anyone to speak to, he would have spoken. But the great gods never showed themselves; they came and they went as they pleased. They knew he had sinned with the little gods. As did he. After such sin, there could be nothing.

He had lost track of the days. He could no longer recall when it had happened, when he had misread the portent of Ai, when the refugees had come and gone.

He had been prepared to fall ill and die at once, but ill-ness had scorned his large body. Now he followed the elders, planting foot ahead of broad foot, step after step after step. They were used to his silences. Out of one of them, perhaps, a prophecy would come at last. Wasn't that why they had taken him along? There was no way they could know that no prophecy was left in him, that he would never prophesy again. They slept, each man by himself, while he alone lay awake.

The skies clouded over again in the night and it began to rain once more, though thinly, with a stingy drizzle. The morning was cheerless. A thick fog covered the mountain, shutting out the world. The elders woke coughing in their cave. Listlessly, they ate the last of the good bread they had brought from Gibeon, casting the leftover crumbs in a corner and covering them with cold ashes. Now nothing was left but the stale bread dotted with mold, the bread of deceit. The cave smelled of mildew and human sleep. It was time to head eastward, toward the desert and the invaders. No one knew when they would encounter them. It could be in a day or in a month. Wrinkled, shivering, gray with morning, they packed their things.

They encountered them almost at once. They had just left the cave, Harsan having prodded Hivai to his feet with a kick, and were descending from the saddle of the ridge in an easterly direction, with fat Divlat bringing up the rear, when they were suddenly surrounded by a band of young men who seemed to have sprung from the bowels of the earth.

None of them heard their captors approach. They were thin and bronzed, a deep color of the sort that never fades, that belonged to the skin itself, more like a layer of desert sand than a suntan. They blinked a little, as if used to greater distances or flatter horizons, and they shivered from the cold. Several of them jumped from foot to foot to keep warm, like large grasshoppers. They were not at all like the local inhabitants.

Impatiently, unsmilingly, as though made rigorous by the morning cold, their captors assailed them with curt questions, one man interrupting another in a Canaanite that was hard to understand. Repeatedly, they inquired about the elders' city, as if guessing that Gibeon was nearby, barely a half-day's walk away.

The elders, however, pretended to know no Canaanite at all. Over and over they pointed to the north with a feigned show of patient rectitude. What city? There was no city. They came from far off, from the north, from the place of the great rivers and great gods. They were Hivites, not Canaanites. Had the Hebrew masters

47

never heard of the Hivites? They were a great people living in the north of the world. They were only sojourning here in Canaan, they were not part of the local populace. No, not at all. They had come from afar with these bundles on their backs, all the provisions they had. Would the Hebrew masters care to see their bread that had gone bad and their worn-out shoes? Look how scratched their feet were—why, there wasn't a thorn or thistle in this whole accursed land that they hadn't stepped on. Who could believe that this bread that was dotted with mold had been still warm when they left home? The Hebrew masters could decide for themselves: would anyone choose to eat bread like this if he could get better?

They talked on and on, gesturing and holding up more proofs—a split waterskin, yet another torn shoe—until their captors finally understood. The young men stood around them, scratching their heads. They had no idea what to do with these unexpected prisoners, who came from no city, village, or even farm worth spying on, but were simply a band of old nomads speaking an incomprehensible tongue. They themselves had been sent ahead to reconnoiter; not a word had been said to them about taking captives, dead or alive.

In the end one of them convinced the others to take the prisoners with them. The elders breathed a sigh of relief. Harsan stealthily nudged Shaham in the ribs: surely the wisest of men, he! But though all had gone well so far, Shaham remained impassive. Crossly he gave the elders a heavy-lidded glance, as if signaling them to be still. The day was still young, and their fate had not yet been sealed. They had better save their breath for later.

All day long they followed their captors. The fog lifted all at once, like a heavy gray blanket raised from the valley, and a warm sun shone down on the world. The Hebrews walked very quickly. The elders could not keep up and fell behind, one of their thin guards circling back each time to berate them for not moving faster. They were being led on a long path that wound through the valleys, keeping their distance from the Jebusite farms visible here and there in the mountains to the south. Perhaps their captors were lost. Indeed, once or twice they recrossed a valley they had already passed through before. They could have gone on in circles forever, round and round, never once climbing a hill to help them get their bearings.

When evening came the Gibeonites collapsed. They could not take one more step. Their breath came in quick gasps; their faces were crimson. It was all they could do to wipe the dusty sweat from their brows and suck the last of the water from their skins. Divlat, who had the most flesh on his bones, lay panting and half-dead.

But once the sun had gone down, the Hebrews were in no hurry either. They simply dropped to the ground, as if despairing of finding shelter for the night. Perhaps they didn't know how to look for it. They threw the elders some bread, which was hardly better than the moldy stuff brought from Gibeon, picked a few pomegranates, on which they sucked loudly, and fell asleep with few words, scattered all over the open field like abandoned belongings. Now and then, wild-haired and groggy with sleep, one of them stirred to drive away a jackal cub that kept approaching too closely, then lay down again like a dead man. It was past midnight when someone managed at last to crack the intruder in the teeth with a club. The animal yelped and vanished.

The Gibeonites huddled together. The moon came and went through tattered clouds, irregularly lighting shrewd old faces that laughed noiselessly into their beards. What fools their captors were. Why, they did not even know how to start a fire. Over and over they had mindlessly tried to kindle it with wet wood, like men who had no knowledge of winter. It was Harsan who had to gather dry twigs of burnet and find a fallen log, from the underside of which good chips could be hacked. It was Ben-Nerbaal who, that morning on the hillside, had to point out a shepherds' well that the Hebrews had passed without noticing. He had shown them how to roll aside the stone and how to draw the water. Why, they were like newborn babes in this mountain land, they and their god together.

They no longer feared the invaders. Their god was not of this country, neither bone of its bone nor flesh of its flesh. They knew they could prevail over him. Gibeon was mightier than any conqueror. With heads held high they would visit the Hebrew camp and speak with dignity; soon the Hebrew god would flee back to the desert he had come from and show his face no more in the land of men. And the invaders would flee with him, like chaff before the wind; from the desert they had come and to the desert they would return. No one would remember either them or their god. The mountain would remain, as always.

Hivai lay alone, as if none of this concerned him. What if the Hebrews came and what if the Hebrews went? The mountain would remain as always. And so would he and his sin. Until the great gods struck him dead.

He paid no attention to Divlat, who rose clutching his chest and groaning in the night, then lay down again and wheezed as if asking for something, perhaps water. For a moment he considered seeing what he wanted, but the thought failed to mobilize his body. Then Divlat's wheezing stopped, and Hivai fell into the sleep, as deep as a pit and as densely submerged as a death, that had overcome him each hour before dawn since the day of the refugees' arrival, a sleep both brief and unrestful.

In the morning Divlat was found dead. Harsan kicked him once or twice, turned him over on his back, and stood regarding him thoughtfully. Then he took out a dagger and cut off the dead man's right hand to present to their captors. The Hebrews looked at the bloody limb and did not know what to do with it. It was, Harsan explained, a token that the prisoner had died on the road, that he had not escaped or been sold into slavery. They were blameless for his death before their masters.

The Hebrews did not understand. At last one of them took the severed hand and flung it into the bushes, wiping his own hand with disgust. A large songbird took off from a bush in low, frightened flight and settled on another bush nearby. The elders looked at each other: had it been up to them, they would have gone to the first bush and searched there for eggs or fledglings. Their captors, however, did not even glance in its direction.

Again they headed eastward. The elders were silent, as if they had spent all their scorn the night before. Short, low clouds flew before the wind, fleeter than they were, as if the real march were taking place up there above the valley. Once, in a sudden, arrogant burst of speed, a Jebusite iron chariot overtook them. Drawn by a black horse, it raced past them from a dirt road on a hillside while they silently, obeisantly made way for it. The Jebusite, his head wrapped in a turban against the wind, cursed them and rode off, spattering mud in the faces of captor and captive alike.

Toward evening they heard many sounds of life, of livestock and camels and people. Around a bend in the road they came upon the Hebrew camp; composed of gray, badly weatherbeaten tents and some hastily constructed wattle huts, it sprawled over a large area. The elders stared at length, narrowing their eyes to slits through which the pupils hardly showed. Even ordinary robbers, even highwaymen, they thought, had finer dwellings than these. And the mindless way the tents were set up, at the very bottom of the valley! All that was needed was one good rain to wash the whole camp away.

A group of men and women came forth to greet the returning scouts, and soon all were part of one embracing, backslapping crowd. The elders tried to look the other way, letting the merriment blow past them.

They stood erect, straightening their cloaks in silence. Each knew what the others were thinking: like conquering heroes, that was how the scouts had been met. What had they conquered? Were they, the elders, such valuable booty that the whole camp turned out to cheer their captors? They stood without moving, as full of contempt as a jug is full of water. The slightest careless motion might send their derision spilling out.

They entered the camp. Their captors quickly vanished in the throng. No one showed the least interest in the four Gibeonites, who were left to fend for themselves.

Hivai, too, raised his eyes to look. The Hebrew camp had an air unlike any he had been in, and he did not know how to breathe it. All around was a great din, the commotion of evening. Children stepped fearlessly up to get a look at them. Tall, laughing women walked right by them with unveiled faces. They had no idea what was expected of them.

In the end they sat down beneath one of several mat awnings scattered haphazardly around the camp, whether tents or merely canopies one could not say. Some mud-caked reed mats lay beneath them for no apparent reason, and on these rested heaps of junk: broken-handled jugs, plucked sprigs of chickpeas, piles of earthenware jars, cabbages, dates, and black, strong-smelling goat wool. Nearby sat a bronzed young woman nursing a child. Bare-faced and bare-breasted, she regarded them curiously, now and then wiping her nose with the corner of her dress. They turned insulted backs on her, contracting themselves with anger.

A second woman sat down by the first and began to converse with her. In her arms she held a small girl about four years old. The girl was crying quietly. From the corners of their eyes they could see a large, swollen abscess on her arm. Her mother collected some old sacks, seated herself upon them, made herself comfortable, and began to blow on the sore. Slowly she cooled it until the girl's crying grew softer and finally stopped altogether; yet still she went on blowing with a soft, soothing rhythm, while the elders shrugged their

shoulders and narrowed their eyes still further, saying
nothing.

Finally, a Hebrew came striding quickly up to them,
and they rose. He was a short, stocky man with small
hands that rose and fell in threshing movements as he
spoke. If they would be so kind as to come with him, he
said in the local language, he would take them to state
their business before Ahilud. He spoke rapidly, with
one swift glance at them, as if that were quite enough.
As they followed him he rubbed his hands with satis-
faction like a man whose affairs are going well. Their
captors, he told them as they walked, had already informed the camp of their skills at hewing wood and
drawing water. Perhaps, he smiled encouragingly,
they would stay on in camp, because there was plenty
of work for them.

They were brought to a tent in which about ten men
were seated, any of whom could have been Ahilud.
Once again they told their story: they were not from
these parts, they were nomads, Hivites from the north,
whose city was very far away; but they were skilled at
all trades and would not deceive the Hebrew masters.

The men in the tent seemed uncertain. Frequently
they paused to consult among themselves, while the
Gibeonites stood stiffly, waiting. In the end several

long sentences were spoken to their stocky guide, who nodded and interpreted for them: the Hebrews would ask the judgment of Joshua, who was two or three days' march away. If the Gibeonites would be so kind as to remain in the meantime, not a hair of their heads would be harmed.

For two whole days they sat on the mat, waiting recumbent, chewing on a bunch of dried dates they had been given. They already knew that the camp was a small and lonely one, and they felt no fear. The air was free, without menace. Sounds of daily life came from everywhere: of cooking, of milking, of work tools, of children at play, and of women singing without hindrance. Even the mother of the girl with the abscess went on blowing on it day and night, as if she had no other work to do.

Thoroughly idle, they passed the time making fun of their captors. Did they think that their children were worth their weight in gold, had they bought them for pieces of silver? The Hebrew husbands must be worn out, their seed must be dry and infertile, for why else would they value each offspring of theirs as if it were an only child? And their wives—as insolent as black goats they were, a flock of goats got from the desert. What manner of men were these, their clothing more ragged than the Gibeonites' fraudulent tatters, leaderless, priestless, elderless? Why, the least slave in Gibeon was a more pleasing sight.

After two days the same stocky fellow came to them again. The camp, he said, was being struck. The messengers to Joshua had not yet returned, but Ahilud said they should proceed with the alliance, because there was no time to wait.

Quickly, without ceremony, they were brought back to the tent they had been in. A few men were seated inside, while four or five youths loitered by the entrance. Once again they were asked who they were and where they came from, and once again they swore they were Hivites from the north. Sojourners they were in Canaan, it was not their home.

The Hebrews barely appeared to be listening; other things were clearly on their minds. Stepping up to the elders, the youths knotted the corners of their cloaks into little foreskins, then did the same to the cloaks of the Hebrews. A man declaimed the words of the ritual in a strange language. Someone else fetched a dagger, tested it with a finger, and cut the knotted corners. The covenant was sealed.

Having unknotted their cloaks, the Gibeonites wished to say a few words, but the Hebrews rushed busily out of the tent, as if the whole matter no longer concerned them. The youths collected the cloth foreskins from the floor and handed several to the Gibeonites for a surety. They tucked the frayed strands of fabric in their belts, the tension draining from their old faces. It was done.

When Shaham, Ben-Nerbaal, and Harsan packed their bundles and set out to inform Gibeon that the siege was over, Hivai stayed behind. Harsan gave him a light kick. In another day or two, he warned, when the Hebrews find out they've been tricked, they'll have your hide. On your feet, fool! Let's go open the gates of the city.

But Hivai stayed where he was. He knew there was no man, beast, or bird in Gibeon that he ever wished to see again.

3

He attached himself to Ahilud's household.

At first he had no idea what his place was or what was expected of him. The Hebrews' customs were strange to him, as was their language; yet the rags he wore, the clothing of deceit, were much like their own dress, and no one paid him any attention. He wandered mutely about the camp, a tall, gangling figure full of humble willingness. When there was a burden to be carried, he carried it; when it was time to feed the few cattle, he fed them. From morning to night he was with the household, made happy by the least nod, gesture, or sign of understanding, which he returned with an exaggerated smile. Still afraid of being made to leave, he clung to the family as though they were his last refuge, sleeping on the edge of the mat, eating whenever anyone remembered to invite him to share the common pot. He never approached without being asked. At times he thought that if an enemy were to attack these people, he would defend them well with all his great strength; then they would love him, and he them. He knew that here and here alone the long arm of the great gods could never reach him.

As if accustomed to the desert, they could not stay long in one place. One morning, nobody knew why or when, they would rise bedraggled and quarrelsome, as if an ill wind had entered their gaunt bodies, dismantle the camp, and move with it to another hill, where once again they set up the same tents and booths. Call it restlessness. On each of these moves, they burdened him with much baggage, since he was a large man. He never complained. Nor did he ask why they kept changing hilltops.

When they discovered Gibeon's ruse, nobody asked for his hide. Perhaps they did not mind what had happened, or perhaps he was too strong and devoted to lose. Possibly, they had even forgotten that he had ever come from Gibeon with the elders. He had become part of the landscape, a man like a tree of the field.

The first winter raged in, deluging the meager camp until there was not a dry spot left or a garment to keep a man warm. All they had was soaked through. Winds battered them day and night, without respite. They stayed in their dripping tents, venturing forth unhappily. Nearly everyone took sick. By now they knew that the valley was a bad place to camp when the torrents of water rushed down from the hills. They knew, too, how to look for shelter in caves and ledges in the hillside. Teeth chattering, trembling from cold, the desert tan grayed from their faces, they promised each other that when winter was done, they would settle down and build good houses.

The main Hebrew camp was far away, and they, sick and rheumy, made no great effort to catch up with it. Sometimes they sent out messengers, who did not always return. Perhaps the ways were impassable, or perhaps the messengers had fallen prey to marauders or to the wild animals that lurked in the dripping bushes. In time, no more were sent.

Hivai lay among them at night, as far from his old home in Gibeon as if there were no such place. A stone house was a thing of the past; so was a food cellar; so were tallow candles in their niches at night and the big-bellied wine and oil jars in their cool lofts. Here nothing came between him and the gray sky, or between his body and the unstable ground, over which, like earth-sweat, brown rivulets of mud flowed ceaselessly between the paths of the camp. Everyone was as caked with it as he was. No one bothered cleaning it off any more. No one wore shoes any more either, because they just weighed a person down. At night they sat around yawning wearily, scraping the mud off their soles, or from between their toes, with whatever implement, stick, or slaughtering knife they could get their hands on, bowed beneath the burden of winter. They talked little. They fell asleep at once.

Of Gibeon he never thought or dreamed. It was as though it were forbidden, a white-hot metal in his memory that would sear him if ever he touched it. Once or twice, dreaming that powerful strangers had come like bailiffs to take him back, he awoke with a cry. He apologized, wanting only to be unobtrusive, afraid to wake them with his troubled sounds. But they, too, often cried out loudly in their sleep.

One morning it snowed, the soft flakes falling like the plumage of doves. There was no sound. The livestock fell silent too, as if soothed by the white hand. The snow wrought a great peace. Frozen and amazed, they stepped out into the stillness, staring at the strange whiteness that had come to rest on tree, stone, and roof, and breathed the all-quiet, all-white air. Not a sound. Not an echo. The palm fronds covering the booths drooped forlornly. It was cold; but the sight of the white sky swirling soundlessly down kept them there for a long time. They tried catching the flakes. They stuck them in their mouths, surprised.

Toward evening the snow turned to hail and everyone ran to escape the fierce barrage. Only the children, fleeing their mothers' arms, danced gleefully about in it, knees red with frost. Their laughter filled the camp. On that white day, the world seemed to rest from all contention. Fear ceased, too. Until the hail ravaged the last of the snow and turned it to ugly little trickles of mud.

Slowly, gradually, Hivai learned their language, word by word, as if cutting it out of stone. His lips encircled the syllables, forming speech as if he were tasting it. Next, he started whispering the words to himself. Finally, in a low voice, he began to speak.

He never alluded to Gibeon. He had excised his former life as though it had never been. He knew very well that the ways of Gibeon would not find favor in these people's eyes. Nor was there any way to explain them. Gibeon was different.

They never inquired about it either. Only once did Marit, Ahilud's wife, ask him what he had been there

before settling among them. She asked in a loud, criti-
cal voice, a frown on her face. She had suspected him
since the day of his arrival, whispering at night to Ahilud that he was a spy, Hivai was, and not to be trusted.
A spy: one day they would all see that she was right.
Now she stood facing him, a wide-hipped woman almost as tall as he was, asking in severe tones. Hesi-
tantly he replied that in Gibeon he had been a prophet.

Marit would not take that for an answer. What, she
wanted to know, had he prophesied there?

Though he knew he should not tell her, he did not
know how to refuse. Perhaps he was unaccustomed to
being questioned by a woman. As sparingly as he
could, he told her about his vision of the drought, about
prophesying the great plague, about knowing in ad-
vance that Yeremoth's father would die.

Marit frowned harder, thought a moment, and declared that this was a seer, not a prophet. How so? he
asked offendedly.

A prophet, she replied, was a man like Moses, who
gave the Law and led the people in the desert. If Hivai
had given Gibeon no law, he was neither a prophet nor
the son of one, but only a seer. And with that she was
off, not waiting for a reply.

It enraged him.

A day or two later, while cutting wood with Ahilud, he inquired discreetly about the Law given by Moses. Was it a secret matter, or could it be discussed? Ahilud seemed perplexed. It was a question, he replied, that had to be asked of those wiser or older than he. He himself had been but a boy when the Law was given in the desert. He had never studied it much. He knew that it forbade a man to murder or to bear false witness. Truly, he did not know much more than that, but everyone knew that the Law was very good.

Hivai humbly begged to be forgiven for his ignorance; but if it was not too much to ask of his lord Ahilud, when was a man forbidden to murder? One could not murder an elder or kill a priest in broad daylight in Gibeon either. Surely, a man would not murder his maternal uncle; in Gibeon, too, it was a transgression.

No, said Ahilud. A man must never murder anyone. That was the law. He could not tell Hivai any more.

Hivai was confused. It was too much for him. He did not ask again.

One way or another, the winter was coming to an end. The constant rush of water that they heard day and night had stopped. Looking eastward across the valley of the Jordan, it was possible to see the mountains on the other side again, a fierce mauve in the sunset. The constant mud was hardening back into earth. Flowers covered the hillsides, red and purple and deep pink; the inner force of the earth burst out, parading its powers in a festive array on slope and bluff. In the Jebusite farms across the valley, men were seen going out to the fields to work the land.

They had no land. Here and there they had carved out tiny plots, scarcely bigger than a man's hand, that they managed to fence off and work: a piece of earth between olive and mastic tree, a few square feet in the valley, or clinging to the side of the hill. They took what they could find: abandoned strips reclaimed by the kingdom of weeds, slopes so steep they could be stood on only by grasping a tree, soil strewn with rocks and stones that no one else on earth would have farmed. They rooted themselves in the mountain as if they were plants themselves, as if a desert wind had sown them by accident and left them to spring up among the boulders, sprouting wherever there was a handful of earth. They learned to leap across the rocks like the goats by their sides, to find their footing in places where even donkeys slipped and fell. They gathered rocks and stones to fashion terraces, leveling the earth with bare hands to keep it from washing away. And there they planted.

Those who found land in the valley below were no better off. Their small yield was soon stolen, whether by the nomadic marauders who cast terror on the countryside, or the Canaanites, or the Jebusites from the mountains. The Jebusites would wait patiently for a crop to ripen, passing it for months as if it were not there, while measuring it with a sideways glance, sure of possession in the end. No sooner had the reaper begun his harvest than they swooped down and made off with it all, leaving behind trampled stubble, broken branches, and tears. There was nothing to do about the Jebusites. They had chariots of iron.

There was much contention in camp. Some said it was foolish to work the land. They were a people of shepherds, and shepherds they would always be, wandering untrammeled from place to place with their flocks. What was the sense in planting trees for others to eat their fruit, or sowing crops for the Jebusite to plunder? Shepherds they were and shepherds they should remain. Their birthplace was the desert, stone houses were not for them; they and their children were meant for mats and booths, free to come and go as they pleased.

Others were silent, as stubborn as the earth itself.

No decision was ever made to stay or move on, yet

each year there were more of those who answered with silence. Perhaps it was the winter that helped make up minds, perhaps the children born in the camp, trembling from the wet and the cold and bleating like baby lambs not long for this world.

They had not the strength to live like that, but also none to decide. Each winter, the first and the second and the third, they told themselves that come spring they would build houses. But they never did. They could not make up their minds. It was not until the fourth year that one or two men gathered large stones and constructed a shelter of them, a rough, solid booth that was not divided into rooms. Others piled stones in a corner and looked at them all summer without building, until once again the winter rains arrived.

Gradually, in the fifth year, stone shelters began to go up. And yet, the Hebrews reassured one another, these were really more tents than houses. They could still come and go as they pleased; they had simply built roofs to keep their children warm and dry.

When spring came, however, they went nowhere. Nor was there anywhere to go. No longer did they live by their flocks alone, but rather grew bread from the earth, glancing up at the sky to see what the prospects for rain were. Backs bent, their vertebrae showed through the dark skin beneath their rags like sharp beads. Calluses covered their hands. They had become one with the mountain, they and their crude dwellings, like vegetation that had pushed up out of the desert and slightly changed the face of the hills. That was all. Yet when sometimes, hot and fierce, a desert wind blew through the camp, they would stand for a moment gazing silently eastward, breathing the wind in deeply, with endless longing.

They themselves could not say when the camp began to have a name. It was no longer just Ahilud's house, or Shirah's house, or Gomer's house, here today and gone tomorrow. From now on the houses on the hill were called Aner, and those in the valley, Eter. No one invented these names. They sprang up by themselves and quickly spread throughout the camp. Perhaps they grew out of the mountain. Suddenly they were there.

White cattle egrets came, too. They walked fearlessly behind the cows, as if they had always been there. And after them arrived an itinerant peddler who, much to the joy of the women, included the camp in his rounds. At harvest time Ahilud's daughters returned from the fields with rings in their ears, their bodies singing. From the hayloft at night came the sound of flutes and the voices of lads and maidens in song.

Hivai did not build a house. He lived in a wattle hut at one end of the land and never visited Ahilud's home. Nor did the family, once it had built a stone house of its own, invite him to eat with them any more. One of the youngsters would bring him out a pot or a large stack of flat, round bread, or else he himself would make a fire and toast the grain he had been allowed to gather. Sometimes, too, Ahilud generously made him a gift of some roast meat or a pinch of dough, or else rewarded him with a coin or some new wool from the shearing. His needs were few.

Marit despised him. Just look at the prophet, she would say, narrowing her eyes. Before you know he'll be prophesying about us, and you can be sure it won't be anything good. Be still, be still, said Ahilud loudly, but she would not be.

Ahilud's sons, though, had no qualms about visiting Hivai. They would come bringing a shoe to be cobbled, a wooden plowshare to be sharpened, a plant to ask if it could be eaten. He had a reputation for being a good workman. Once he even took some reeds they had brought and made them some fine flutes. They thanked him with a rough pat on the shoulder and forgot him the moment they left him, as though he himself were but another of their tools.

He was not at peace. When the day's work was done and it was time to go home, they to their house and he to his hut, the thoughts came thick and fast. He had worked for them for seven years, which now seemed like one long, laborious day. Not once had he failed them, not for a moment had he left the camp or stopped cutting wood, fetching water, and faithfully doing his chores. And yet he was still as much an outsider as ever, unversed in their Law, walking the same straight line every day from the fields to his hut and from his hut to the fields. True, their god had kept his word: as long as Hivai lived in their midst, he was protected. The great gods had not come to wreak vengeance. He was alive and well. The god of the Hebrews dealt honestly and had neither cheated nor betrayed him. Yet neither had he revealed himself. Though Hivai would gladly have brought him a thanksoffering, the god had eluded him.

He thought and he thought, and the more he thought the bitterer it made him. He could feel his gorge rise. Was he a leper or a woman in her menses that he should not be allowed to worship their god with them? He had served them faithfully, and they had let him down. Never once had he seen their god. Was he big or small? Did he speak with a man's voice or a woman's? They had built houses, too, and hidden the sacrifice, as if he were unworthy of seeing it. They had even told him there was none, which was nothing but a mealymouthed lie. Could a house be built without blood being spilled and a victim laid under the cornerstone? He was not a gullible child. They were keeping things from him, they were leading him astray and not letting him pay his debts to their god. Against his will they had made him an ingrate and a stranger.

His sense of injustice grew from day to day. He was a prophet, not a slave, and he would see their god. He would bow down to him and prophesy in his name, faithfully, as he had done long ago, and all the Hebrews would listen. They alone stood between him and their god, as if he were a dark secret. But he would find him; he would study the Law, and regain his old powers, and prophesy. They and they alone kept him from his true vocation.

One day in the field he asked Ahilud, but he couldn't get a straight answer. Their God, said Ahilud, had no form or body or shape. No man could see him and live, except perhaps Moses. That was the truth of it, even if he, Ahilud, did not entirely understand. But he was the same God who had taken them out of the land of Egypt, and given the earth to men, and given a Law upon the earth, for which he held them accountable.

Hivai persisted. But if your god has no body, he asked, how did he smite all the other gods? To which Ahilud answered curtly that there were no other gods.

He knew now for sure that he was being mocked. If they would not show him their god—if they had hidden him away in some shed, sack, or pit—he, Hivai, would have to go find him himself. And find him he would, and bring him a thanksoffering, and so be one of them at last.

Night after night, wrapped in his cloak, he stole out of his shack to prowl about the camp. Unseen, he foraged in old sacks, poked through piles of belongings, peered under plaits of onions, garlic, and beans, a man in search of god. He slipped past the snores of the sleepers and the sudden wingbeats of fowl that awoke briefly and then went back to sleep.

He kept it up for weeks. And yet, as if the desert had purged them of it all, he did not find a thing: not one image, statue, or idol. Not even an altar, or a stone hollowed for the blood. He flitted across the darkness, briefly silhouetted in the moonlit space between the

74

houses before merging with the stone walls again. Not until a first pallor streaked the sky did he return to his hut, his heart beating hard.

And then one night he was caught. In the bright moonlight flooding the camp, a man had stepped outside to void himself. Squatting in the shadow of a wall, he saw Hivai's large figure start to slip away. When the man grabbed him, Hivai sought to break the man's grip. He was bigger than his pursuer, and the two were soon panting from exertion and fear. Catching hold of the hand that grasped him, he snapped the bones of several fingers and fled.

The shouts brought everyone running. They found him trembling, hiding behind the threadbare rugs in his hut. Their harsh voices sounded angry, betrayed. Marit stood triumphantly in her doorway, slowly running her hands over her hips. They would have thrashed him soundly on the spot had not Ahilud declared that justice was meted out by day, not by night. And so, tying him to a post, they went back to sleep.

In the morning three men brought him to the place of the trial. He stood there in sullen submission, not even trying to explain. He knew they would only laugh at him, mocking and incredulous. He knew, too, that they would cut off his right hand, as was the custom of the land. They were strong, he was weak, and justice was theirs. He did not even have a god in this place to defend him.

He awaited his judge. About a dozen men and women stood waiting too. He was sure the judge would be Ahilud, since it was his household he belonged to. Yet the man who came in the end was not Ahilud but Shirah. There was a hush when he appeared.

Shirah asked Hivai's accuser what it was that Hivai had stolen and tried hiding among his own possessions. Was it some bread? An article of clothing? Provisions of some sort? The man replied that naught had been stolen. The Gibeonite had taken nothing, for he had been timely discovered. Then, said Shirah, if no thing was taken, what punishment is due? You yourself say he stole not.

The onlookers nodded, exchanging whispers. Shirah's words were spoken truly. The Gibeonite had not stolen and therefore could not be punished. The verdict was just.

But Hivai's accuser was adamant. The Gibeonite has a wicked heart, he cried, holding up his hand to the crowd. Here, he broke these two fingers; he did it deliberately. The man is an evildoer.

Shirah asked the Hebrew if Hivai had lain in wait to kill him or break his fingers. No, said the man, it had happened while they were wrestling. But now his fingers were broken and he could not use them until the bones knit. Was it right that there be no indemnity?

There shall be indemnity, said Shirah. Let him pay you two kessita coins, a coin for each finger, for it happened while you wrestled. And now go home, both of you, for there is no blame in either.

All that day Hivai kept to his hut, like one who was ill. Now and then he stared at his right hand, as if to make sure that it was really there. He made a fist and opened it, made it again and slowly opened it once more, unable to believe his own fingers.

That evening Ahilud came to see him, sitting next to him on the rugs. Hemming and hawing with embarrassment, he told Hivai that there was no better worker than he in all Aner. But Marit did not approve of him; she insisted he go away. Though for years he, Ahilud, had stood firm as a rock against her, he was not young any more; he was gray in the face from her complaints and no longer had the strength to resist. And besides, from now on every missing piece of string would be blamed on him by Marit, who would want to know how much longer she must put up with him. He, Ahilud, knew very well that Hivai had never laid a hand on anything. Not one straw, not one thread in his hut came from anyone else's kine, chattel, or land. There was not a more honest man in the village, and he, Ahilud, would deal honestly too, he would not take advantage of Hivai; no, he would pay him his full wage and even more; he would give him a suit of clothes and ten kessitas and a pair of good shoes, for he had served them faithfully for seven years. Let there be no bad blood between them.

Hivai nodded. Ahilud had spoken well. Hivai himself had thought to depart long ago, yet each time he had decided to sojourn a while longer, and lo, seven years had gone by. In the morning he would pack his things and go. Truly, Ahilud had taken no advantage and had done him no wrong. And he, Hivai, had served him faithfully, so that the convenant had been kept.

He fumbled in his belt and produced some scraps of cloth that were left from the day the covenant was sealed. Ahilud stared at them with emotion. He touched the faded bits of fabric. I have kept the words of the covenant, he said to Hivai. So you have, Hivai said to him. They looked at each other. The day the covenant was sealed their hair had been black, and now it was the hair of old men.

Ahilud's grandchildren walked him to the road. They waved to him. Good-bye, Hivai, they called, good-bye, Hivai.

He did not look back.

4

Hivai headed westward.

He walked slowly. He was not in any hurry. At first he bore the camp with him, still full of its sights and sounds. Something akin to sorrow, or at least to a sense of grievance, refused to go away. For seven years he had served them; he had taught them every trade and craft of the land; yet he had learned nothing from them in return. True, they had given him a just trial, and they had kept the words of the covenant. Yet there was something they had withheld from him, though he could not say what it was. He was leaving them the same man he had come. Seven years had passed as one day. Nothing had happened. A Gibeonite he had been, and a Gibeonite he still was.

Slowly, step by step, he began to regard his route

more closely. The day seemed old and gray, although he could not say if what had aged was himself or the weary earth. The trees bore their fruit bleakly and the few flowers on the hillsides had a dull, gnawed look. The mountains and the sky lacked luster; the air was close, an unlifting cloud of grief.

A well-trodden path ran through the valley. Hivai was not alone on it. A man passed leading a donkey, on whose bolster sat a woman with a large fardel of twigs that stuck out on both sides. Some persons carrying a burden came toward him quickly, almost on the run. For seven years he had not descended from the mountain, and now here was this road and here were all these people.

The war had gone before him. Here and there by the roadside stood ruined houses and dead fruit trees with charred trunks and yellowed leaves. Once or twice he had to outwalk the smell of a corpse. He had no idea who had lived in these houses or who had destroyed them. He had no idea why the mountains looked so bleak.

Toward evening on the second day, as the sun was setting, he saw houses by the road. There were not enough of them to be a village. Several cows stood tethered to a trough, mooing at it softly, their hooves slithering on the wet ground. The fruit trees looked better here: there were figs and pomegranates, and a booth trellised with grapevines, from which hung heavy clusters of fruit. From inside what he realized was a breeding shed came a sound of bellowing. Several youths opened a wide door, through which they tried to pull a big black bull; its feet bound, its back muscles arched like a bridge, the animal lowered its head to the ground and refused to budge. A wreath of wilted laurel leaves hung from its neck.

Hivai stepped up and helped them pull the bull outside, holding it by its nose-ring. The boys thanked him, joking among themselves. He's already mounted eight cows, they explained in Canaanite, and he still wants more. He's a stud of studs, he was bought up north. You can't find bulls like him around here. Proudly, they kicked him a bit.

Hivai asked if there was anywhere nearby where he might find food and lodging. They pointed to a house among some trees. Let the traveler follow the smoke and the smells and they would bring him to the yard of an inn.

He entered, ducking his large head as he stepped through the doorway. The room was dark and smelled of wine and mutton. Hivai felt very hungry. Seating himself on a rug, he put down his pack. Three or four men were seated in the dim light at the other end of the room, gnawing on some bones before throwing them to a waiting dog that leaped up in the air to catch them, stretching its body string-taut and retracting it over its prize.

He sat resting for a while until a youth of about seventeen approached him with a basin of water. The boy's chest, which glistened with oil, was bare except for some black leather straps. More straps bound his arms. He walked like a dancer.

The boy knelt in front of Hivai and washed his feet, talking all the while. Surely the guest was weary from walking the mountains, he would feel better once his feet were washed and oiled. And should the guest want a woman, there was a harlot nearby, under the oak tree not far from the inn.

Hivai shook his head. He was too old, he said, his strength was no longer what it used to be. He hadn't had a woman in years. He shut his eyes as the hands massaged the soles of his feet, feeling his whole body relax. Perhaps tomorrow or the day after, he thought vaguely, he might visit the harlot after all to see if his strength was still with him.

While Hivai made himself comfortable, the youth

took away the basin and returned with a pitcher of wine and some mutton and lentil stew. He stood by to serve him, balancing lightly on his feet and inquiring where the guest was from. He was a Gibeonite, said Hivai, though he had not been in that city for years and was now just passing through the land.

The youth's eyes lit up. Gibeon, he said reverently, was a city of brave warriors; he would like nothing better than to join them one day when he was a man. There was not another city like it among the kingdoms of the earth. The others had all been defeated, they had gone down like grass before that locust come from the desert; only Gibeon had resisted, unharmed despite its long siege. It had fought well and prevailed. He spoke with admiration, valiantly flexing his strapped biceps, his bare chest glistening with oil.

Hivai asked when all this had happened. That, said the youth proudly, was something he could tell him exactly: it had happened seven years ago. A great enemy had laid siege to Gibeon, but the city's gates had remained shut and it had held out. There had been traitors too, he could tell the guest about them also, there had been traitors in the city who were killed.

Who were the traitors? asked Hivai. He could not remember all their names, said the boy, dancing about on his feet, but one of them was even a judge. Shahar his name was, or Shaham, and another was called Yerubaal. Or perhaps it was Nerbaal. He would go ask his father, no one knew better than he. And there had been a prophet too, a great traitor, who had deserted to that abomination of a people, the Hebrews, and joined the enemies of his own city. It had been wise of the king to put him to death along with the treacherous elders. Might that be the fate of all enemies.

And what was the king's name? asked Hivai. He did not know the king's name, replied the youth, but when he had been in Gibeon at harvest time with all his father's house, he had seen him standing by the great pool; he was an albino, with a very red face. If the guest wished for more wine or bread he need only ask for it; it was a great honor to wait on one of the Gibeonites, whose bravery was famed throughout the land.

Hivai sat musing over his wine for a long while. The three men at the other end of the room kept drinking and talking in low voices; they laughed in low tones too, and then began to sing an unfamiliar ditty while slapping each other sottishly on the back. Hivai could not make out their faces in the darkness. They were sitting too far away and they never once looked in his direction.

The room grew darker. The youth returned with a large bundle of rolled-up rugs, spread them for the guests along the walls, and smoothed them out. Hivai lay down on his back, cradling his head in his hands. A solitary candle flickered in a wall niche, throwing a long shadow; then someone rose and blew it out.

Why, then, I am a dead man, thought Hivai in the darkness.

Morning found him ashen-faced outside the inn. He knew he could not stay in this place, yet he had nowhere to go. He was neither Gibeonite nor Hebrew. He was an outcast in the mountains, with nowhere to return to, no people, no city, no god. How great indeed must be his sin.

He walked on, dragging his feet. The road had already been taken by the war. Yet though the earth was still black from fire, here and there strong new shoots sprouted from dead tree trunks and outbursts of green patched the charred ground. The mountain was fighting back, the verdant life within it stubbornly bursting forth, trying to cover the ashes as if nothing had happened, as if there had been no devastation at all.

He had no idea how long he walked, carrying his pack on his back. Sometimes it seemed that it was all just one indeterminably long, exhausting dream before a morning that must come to find him in the end back in his old house in Gibeon, or on Ahilud's land. But the harsh dream went on and on. The road was well traveled; many people passed by on foot, sometimes leading beasts of burden; yet he scarcely bothered to look at them. What was there to see? Life for him was something that was over.

I am old, Hivai thought. An old man. And the gods of this country are all dead.

Toward evening he arrived at a crossroads. Some people were walking toward him, and he asked them where the main road led. It is the old road to Ai, they told him. The city is not far, though there is nothing there but ruins and some dwellers in the ruins. You won't find an inn there, or even a crust of good bread, because the ruin dwellers are dirt-poor.

He headed for Ai. It was almost dark when he arrived. The toothed wall of the city was still intact in parts, its jagged outline dark against the evening sky. No end of rubble lay on the slope beneath it: broken houses, broken roofs, broken stone, broken brick, broken clay, broken tile, broken glass clouded over and sightless. Here and there in this city of breakage burned little fires, over which families warmed their suppers.

He sat down on the rubble, which felt warm from the afternoon sun. Each time he moved or changed position the pile shifted under him, or brought new wreckage tumbling from above. There was no end of it. He took out the last wad of dried dates he had brought from Aner, tore off a handful of them, and began to eat.

After a while he was approached by a woman with a candle. Please, sir, she said, it would be a great honor if you joined my husband and sons and shared our meal with us. And bless you if you could give the little ones a few of those dates, because they haven't tasted a sweet in many a day.

She lit his way in the darkness here and there to keep him from stumbling. The family greeted him warmly. They were simple people.

He distributed the last of his dates to his hosts, who sucked on them slowly, careful not to swallow them too soon. They smiled at him.

Who had destroyed the mighty city of Ai? he asked the head of the family. Why ask, brother, answered the man, when we ourselves have forgotten. Six different times Ai was destroyed. A curse was upon it; there was no enemy or invader who did not level it anew, the Canaanite and the Amorite and anyone else you can

88

name. It was each man against his brother on this mountain.

Hivai asked if the Hebrews had been there too. Yes, said the man. They were here and moved on. They fought treacherously, luring the defenders outside the gates and attacking them on open ground. But it was not they who destroyed the walls, he went on. The Hebrews are not a strong people, they come and go like locusts. It was the Amorites, they and their battering rams. But why sit speaking of the war? The war was there for all to see. No one was left in this entire city of ruins but themselves and a few other households, though perhaps the town might be rebuilt, since the countryside had survived. Behold, there was even a bit of green here and there, and perhaps the trees would once more give their fruit. Truly, where else could they go? There was no place for them anywhere on the mountain. They would stay where they were and hope for better times.

They went on talking for a while, the children staring at the newcomer until their eyes shut, after which all lay down to sleep on the rubble. Hivai rested his head on his bundle, watching the faraway stars wheel slowly through the sky.

That night Sahali came to him. Not the young woman he had sent off to Ai, but a small child, almost an infant. She looked at him with blazing eyes, hating him with all her might.

Why did she hate him so? he asked in wonderment. Had he not been good to her? Had he not bought her rings and anklets? Had he not sent her off to safety with an escort? Why, they both were dead now, she a dead child and he a dead prophet: how could the dead hate the dead?

But she went on sitting there and staring at him, hard and angular, her every word a curse. You spent your whole life making up to the gods, she mocked. The gods were all you ever cared about.

But against whom else can a man sin? he asked uncomprehendingly.

She rose and shouted at him that he did not understand a thing. Not one thing, she screamed, and was gone.

He felt a great weight bearing down on him.

When he rose in the morning everyone was asleep, each where he had lain down. They did not hear him leave. They were used to the crunch of footsteps on the rubble and were not awakened by them.

He was heading east now, with no way to get rid of

the weeping building up inside him. His feet kept going by themselves, taking him ever eastward.

At last he reached a hill overlooking the Jordan. On his right was a high cliff, covered with scrub on its west side, steep and arid where it faced the river. Down below, the river snaked back and forth, its banks dark with palm trees, a luxuriant thicket of green.

He descended to the rift of the Jordan. Between cliff and water lay a strip of bright sand, beyond which stood a thicket by the bank. There was not a human soul, just the trill of many songbirds in the treetops. The river blocked him one way, the cliff another. A ponderous heat oppressed the valley.

He cut some palm fronds, spread his cloak upon a branch, and made himself a shelter to rest in. He would go no further, he told himself, because he had nowhere further to go. He was an old man. A dead man. A fleeting shadow. No deed ever done by him upon the earth had done the least bit of good. Here let him live a while longer, here let him die, and here let his trials be over.

The place was good to him. A bit up the cliff pheasants could be snared, and he laid out some animal traps too, though he rarely trapped anything big enough to eat. Sometimes he went down to the river, rolled up his sleeves, and fished with both hands. In time, peeling the fibers from the palm fronds, he learned to weave them into nets. Evenings were for resting, or for watching the mountains of Moab across the river turn purple and scarlet in the sunset. It was a godforsaken existence, and he liked it that way.

After a year or two he noticed that the traps had been empty for some time. At first he blamed the traps: they needed repair, the prey was getting away. But though he mended each of them, in the morning, when he went from trap to trap in the thick brush, the pits were empty and their concealment of twigs had been disturbed. It puzzled him greatly.

One day, as he was making his way through the thicket, he heard a sharp whistle close by. Looking up in alarm, he spied a small boy of seven or eight sitting half-naked in a hawthorn tree with a shepherd's pipe in his mouth. When he saw that he had been noticed, the boy leaned forward and whistled loudly again, right into Hivai's ear.

Hivai felt a wave of anger. The boy was teasing him, holding him up to ridicule like the clowning children in Gibeon. Their derision had followed him even here, to find him and destroy his peace of mind.

Blind with rage, he pulled the boy from the tree and cast him down by the throat with both hands. The boy stammered wordlessly, and when he opened his mouth to catch his breath, Hivai saw he had no tongue. It must have been cut out in one of the wars.

He released the boy, who jumped back on his feet at once and ran off with a heavy, muffled whimper, turning as he fled to pelt Hivai with branches, pebbles, dirt, whatever he could lay his hands on.

He knew now who had been stealing from his traps. Walking back to his shelter of palms, he sat down to think.

About a month later he saw the tongueless boy again. He was kneeling by one of the traps, inspecting its sharp stakes. His thin legs tensed to spring away as he heard Hivai approach, but Hivai called out that he would do him no harm.

The boy stood a ways off, his legs still poised for flight, his thin body breathing heavily. He was sunken-eyed and sickly looking. Hivai threw him a waterskin, which landed next to him. Afraid to bend down, he nudged it away with his foot, kicking it further and further until he judged the distance was safe. Even as he stood pouring water over his back, his eyes, dark with fright, never left Hivai for a moment.

Hivai told the boy to follow him to his shelter. Without waiting to see if he did, he turned around and walked ahead, tramping through the dry leaves on the sand. He could hear the boy's footsteps behind him, stopping and starting again.

But the boy was afraid to enter the shelter. A few feet from it he balked and ran away.

Not long afterward, Hivai heard steps in the leaves. The boy was in the doorway, looking too weak to either stand or sit. In the end he pitched forward, falling face down in the sand. His back was covered with infections and scratches where, driven crazy by the itching, he had scraped himself on the trunks of trees.

Hivai poured water over the feverish back. The boy shivered wordlessly.

That night the boy ran a fever and was delirious, emitting the heavy grunts of a mute. Hivai lay close by without moving. This one too will die, he thought, and wherefore then am I? He thought of finding a willow tree and decocting a salve from its leaves, but the idea seemed somehow shameful. Was he a Hebrew woman to sit blowing on a child's back? The boy would either live or die.

In the morning he was alive, though very pale. Hivai set out food between them. The boy would not eat, but he drank and drank with eager gulps. Then he put his pipe in his mouth, whistled a feeble thank you once or twice, and fell asleep. He slept all that day and all that night.

The next morning he was gone.

Once again Hivai was alone. The nights in the rift valley were getting cold; clouds from the west sailed overhead. Across the river the mountains of Moab were lost in the first light rain. One day he made up his mind and set out, climbing back into the mountains, into the land of men.

After two or three days he found a flock with its shepherd. They haggled at length. Hivai did not have many coins left in his belt and the shepherd was stubborn. He drove a hard bargain, even rounding up his flock and walking off while Hivai followed pleadingly after him.

In the end they split the difference. Hivai bought a pregnant ewe and a pair of goats. He tied them together with a rope and headed back for his shelter.

The boy was sitting in the doorway when he arrived. He jumped to his feet when he saw Hivai, piping short, high whistles of joy; then, spying the goats and the sheep, he blew with all his breath one more, very long whistle of excitement. Sternly, Hivai made him stop. Instead of deafening a person, why didn't he make himself useful and untie the tired animals and water them? He even gave the boy a name: Gosha. At first he didn't know why. Then suddenly, as if an intricate knot had slipped open inside him, he remembered: why, that was the name of his brother, his little brother who had been sacrificed before his eyes in the temple in Gibeon, cast into the flames when he wasn't yet five years old. He must have always known that name, must have remembered it all along.

The boy Gosha didn't seem to mind. Perhaps it really was his name, or perhaps he just happened to like it. He lingered a while in the shelter, feeding the ewe and the goats while making little noises to himself, and ran off. Hivai noticed that in his absence the boy had stolen a rug. He swore a bit but hadn't the strength to be angry. The trip had exhausted him.

Each morning he descended to the river to fill the waterskins, walking slowly because his old legs were not so spry any more. The evening chills made every joint ache. He had to force himself to wade into the water in order to pull in the nets. At night he made a fire and huddled close to it, his legs hurting him no matter how still he lay.

Prophecy returned to him too, the small, harmless prognostications of old men. He knew when it would rain on the mountains across the river, funneling down from the gray storm clouds. He knew which date palm would bear the first fruit, and what he would find when he opened his traps, a lizard, mouse, or jackal cub. They pleased him, these prophecies, like small, humble blessings. Once he dreamed of the great pool in Gibeon, but felt no fear. He knew he would never return.

When Gosha came to visit he chided him cantankerously, like an old man. In reply the boy merely grunted. He must make sure to come down with him to the river each morning, said Hivai, because he was too old to carry the waterskins and empty the nets by himself. How long would Gosha eat the bread of idleness and go on stealing from the traps? He knew the boy's evil ways and manners; if Gosha would not help him each morning, let him not set foot in the shelter.

Gosha listened stolidly, then turned and went. It was not for him.

Yet one morning he was there, leaning on a stick and piping short whistles to call Hivai. Without a word the two went down to the river.

After that, he came every morning. The ewe gave birth in the spring. The boy was fond of her milk, sometimes stealing it from the lambs and guzzling it before their eyes. Their trips to the river took a long time, for

Hivai's legs could barely carry him. He leaned on the boy both going and coming, careful not to hurt his old scars. Once he cut some good reeds by the river, brought them back to the shelter, and threw them in a corner among some pots and rags.

The sunsets turned the mountains of Moab to gold in a broad flood of light that spanned both horizons over mountain and water and copses of tall palms. They sat watching while the light retreated slowly up the mountain, gathering the train of its radiant dress, and the earth of the valley released the day's heat with a smell of bulrushes and fish and much water.

Perhaps next winter, he told the boy Gosha, perhaps even this year, he would take the good reeds and make them both flutes.

Design by David Bullen
Typeset in Mergenthaler Palatino
by Wilsted & Taylor
Printed by Arcata Graphics/Fairfield
on acid-free paper